Megan's Journey

By Janet Peel

Megan's Journey

Copyright © Janet Peel 2016 All Rights Reserved

The rights of Janet Peel to be identified as the author of this work have been asserted in accordance with the Copyright, Designs and Patents Act 1988

Spiderwize
Remus House
Coltsfoot Drive
Woodston
Peterborough
PE2 9BF

www.spiderwize.com

A CIP catalogue record for this book is available from the British Library.

The views expressed in this work are solely those of the author and do not necessarily reflect the views of the publisher, and the publisher hereby disclaims any responsibility for them.

All characters in this publication are fictitious and any resemblances to real people either living or dead are purely coincidental.

ISBN: 978-1-911113-81-2

For Dad,
and his 'White Wonders'
Trixie, Mandy, Max and Megan
Always loved, never forgotten

Acknowledgements

A massive thank you to Lily Bolland, Asha Zahran, Aliya Zahran, Alexia Hope Rixon, Warren Bennett, Fynn Kennedy, Hope Kennedy, Megan Lees, Joel Gough and Stan Gough - my Mini Reviewers, who read, loved, understood and gave excellent feedback when Megan's Journey was in its very early stages. Thanks for helping me see things through your eyes, so that I could write Megan's Journey for other children to love, just as much as you did.

Thanks to everyone at Spiderwize - particularly Haylee. Thanks to Paul Crowther for always taking the very best care of our Westies. Big thanks to the Poppy World family - your love and support knows no bounds. Big love as ever to Marc for encouraging me to believe Megan's Journey could become a reality, and extra special love, to my wonderful Mum, without who none of this would have been possible.

And to Poppy, the cheekiest, noisiest, funniest, most lovable and beautiful little Westie, who came into our lives at a time when our hearts were broken and sad after losing Megan. Pops, you have filled us up with more love and sunshine than you will ever know, and even though you are a cheeky monster, you are loved more and more every day. You have proved that life and love go on, and that hearts don't have to stay broken forever.

Megan the Westie was snuggled asleep, comfortable and warm, when she heard an unfamiliar voice speak her name.

"Wake up Megan, wake up little one," the voice said.

Megan thought she was dreaming, and settled back down for more sleep. And then she felt a gentle paw touch her head.

"Megan, it's time to wake up, you have arrived."

Megan slowly opened her eyes and lifted her head and looked around to see the most beautiful place she had ever seen. It was like the park where she had her walks with Mummy, Daddy, Poppy and Louie, but it was twinkling, as though delicate stars were dancing on the branches of the trees and on the blades of grass.

"Are you okay?" said that unfamiliar voice, and Megan turned to see a huge dog, a St Bernard she thought, sitting beside her. "My name is Jessie," the large dog said, "and it is my job to welcome you today and to make you feel at home."

Megan was confused. 'This is not my home,' she thought, 'my home is with my family.' She looked at Jessie and said, "Where are Mummy and Daddy? Where are Poppy and Louie? They don't like me running off, they will be worried."

Jessie stretched her huge paw towards Megan and gently rested it upon Megan's back. "Your mummy and daddy know where you are, Megan." Again Megan was confused. Her mummy and daddy had never let her out of their sight before, and surely Daddy would be wanting his afternoon sleepy cuddles with her. She knew she had to get back. She didn't want to get into trouble for being away from home.

Megan moved to get up, but her body felt tired and her legs felt wobbly. She sat back down and began to cry. She didn't like being away from home, and because Megan was a doggy who loved her food, her tummy was rumbling and she knew that it must be dinner time soon.

"I'm scared," sobbed Megan. "I don't know where I am, and I want to go home." She lay down on the floor and buried her face in her paws. "I don't know anyone here," she cried. "I don't understand."

Jessie lay down beside Megan on the grass and said, "Would you like me to tell you a story?" Megan's tired little body snuggled into the side of Jessie, and she closed her eyes and Jessie began.

Once upon a time there were two little Westies called Max and Megan. They played together, and loved each other, and neither could imagine life without the other. Megan was lazy and liked to snooze the day away with her daddy, or sit and watch Poppy and Louie, her human sister and brother, play with their toys. Max was far from lazy, he was a bouncy, fun-loving Westie who loved to play with his ball with Louie, or run off with Poppy's dolls in his mouth to bury them in the garden. He also liked to bark at everyone passing by the house, and he especially liked to bark at the postman. At night, Megan and Max snuggled together in their bed, and kept each other warm and safe.

One day, Max didn't feel very well and didn't want to play. Megan didn't understand why, and she noticed that Mummy and Daddy were worried. "Would you like to play, Max?" Megan asked him, but he shook his head and said, "No, sorry Megan, I'm just too tired."

Louie threw his ball for Max, but Max just lay in his bed quiet and sad. "Why won't Max play with me?" Louie asked Daddy.

"He's not feeling very well," said Daddy, "best to just let him rest."

A few days later, Megan sat in the window with Daddy as Mummy took Max out in the car. Megan was still sat in the window when Mummy came home without Max. 'Where is he?' she thought, and when Mummy and Daddy hugged each other and cried, she climbed onto Mummy's knee and kissed away her tears.

When Poppy and Louie came home from school, Mummy and Daddy sat them down and told them that Max had gone to live at Rainbow Bridge, and they all cuddled together and cried. "I miss Max," cried Poppy.

"Me too," cried Louie.

'Rainbow Bridge?' thought Megan. 'Where is that? I've never heard of Rainbow Bridge.' Sensing the confused look on her face, Mummy hugged her close and said, "It's where all the special doggies go when they are old or poorly and can no longer live at home."

Mummy and Daddy cried for days after Max had gone to Rainbow Bridge, and Poppy and Louie were very sad too. Megan gave them all the kisses and cuddles they needed to make them feel better. She was sad that Max had gone, but thought that if Mummy and Daddy had let Max go to live at Rainbow Bridge, then it must be a very special place. Max was their best boy, so she decided that Rainbow Bridge must be for all the extra special doggies.

Months passed, and although Max was always missed, Mummy and Daddy began to smile again, and the house was filled with the laughter of Poppy and Louie playing together. Mummy placed a photograph of Max on the fireplace and every night Daddy would lift it up and say "Hello my lad."

Megan noticed that Mummy placed white feathers beside Max's photograph, and every time she put a new one on the pile, Mummy said, "Thank you little man." When they went on walks to the park, Megan noticed that Poppy and Louie also collected small white feathers from the ground, and when they got home they went to place them beside Max's photograph.

Nobody mentioned Rainbow Bridge again, but Megan decided that if Rainbow Bridge was a place for extra special doggies, then maybe one day, if she was a very good girl, she might be able to go there too.

As the years went by, Megan continued to be a good girl, but she was older now, and sometimes her little legs felt so weak and wobbly that she didn't really want to go for walks. She would park her fluffy bottom on the floor and look at Mummy as if to say, "I'm not sure I can go for a walk today." Daddy had also become older, and his legs didn't work too well either, so in the end, rather than going for a walk, Mummy said they would walk around the garden instead. It was a big garden, and as Megan plodded along, sniffing the flowers and the grass, Mummy and Daddy walked beside her.

Poppy and Louie had grown too, and they didn't play with their toys any more. Instead they liked to sit with Megan on the sofa and watch television together.

One day, Megan didn't feel very well and it was an effort for her to walk. All she wanted to do was sit on Mummy's knee, or snuggle with Daddy and sleep through the afternoon. Megan was tired and felt sad, and she wondered whether this was how Max had felt when he didn't want to play or go for walks any more. She remembered that he'd gone to that place, now what was it called? She couldn't think of the name, but then she heard Mummy talking to Daddy in the kitchen. They were talking about letting Megan go and live at Rainbow Bridge.

Megan was filled with a mixture of sadness and curiosity. Going to Rainbow Bridge meant that she would see Max again, but it also meant that she would no longer see Mummy and Daddy and Poppy and Louie again, and that saying goodbye would make them cry. She was torn between staying with her family, but feeling old and slow and unable to play, or heading off on a journey to the mysterious Rainbow Bridge to find Max. She would be so sad to leave everyone behind, but she would be so happy to see Max again.

The next night, Megan became very poorly and she was very tired and weary. Mummy and Daddy hugged her close and sat with her through the night, telling her that soon she would no longer feel pain, because soon she would be running through big, bright fields with Max and would feel as young and as happy as she had when she was a little girl. Poppy and Louie kissed her furry head before they went to bed. "Night night, Megan," they said.

Megan thought Mummy and Daddy were so brave. 'They love me so much,' she thought, 'but they also know I have missed Max, and they want us to play together again.' Megan smiled as she snuggled further into Mummy. 'That's love, that is,' thought Megan, and she drifted back off to sleep.

The next day Poppy and Louie kissed Megan goodbye before they went to school. Mummy then took Megan for a ride in the car. They said goodbye to Daddy, and he kissed Megan's head and said, "I love you, old girl." The ride in the car was short, and soon they were sat talking to Uncle Paul, the vet man. Megan was confused. She liked Uncle Paul the vet man, but she wasn't sure why she had to come and say bye-bye to him too before she went to Rainbow Bridge. She was too tired to give him a kiss goodbye, so instead, she curled in Mummy's arms, and Uncle Paul the vet man stroked her head, and she felt relaxed and calm.

"It's time to go and find Max now sweetheart," Mummy said, and she placed a kiss on Megan's head. Uncle Paul the vet man told Megan she was going to have a lovely big sleep, and when she woke up she would be at Rainbow Bridge. Megan took one last look at Mummy, who had tears streaming down her face. 'Don't cry Mummy,' thought Megan, 'I will see you again...'

"That's me," said Megan as she woke from her slumber with a start. "That's me in the story." She wiped the sleep from her eyes and took another look at her surroundings. "Am I at Rainbow Bridge?" she asked Jessie. "Is that really where I am?"

And then she saw him in the distance, getting closer and closer. "Megan!!" he shouted, as he bounced through the grass. "Megan, I can't believe you're here." As Max approached, Megan found herself suddenly full of life. Her legs felt like they worked again, and as she bounced up to meet Max she felt lighter and happier and younger than she had done for years.

"Max!!" she squealed, and they jumped up and down on each other and rolled in the grass like they had all those years ago. "It's so good to see you, I have missed you so much." Jessie sat back and smiled as the two dogs re-lived memories of the fun they had shared together. And then Megan stopped jumping and sat down, and she started to cry. "But if I'm at Rainbow Bridge it means I'm never going to see Mummy and Daddy and Poppy and Louie again. I miss them and want them to know that I got here safe." She slumped on the grass and cried.

"It's okay," said Max, "just because you are at Rainbow Bridge, it doesn't mean that you can't see them all, because you can."

Megan looked up. "I can?" she said, sniffing through her tears.

"Yes you can," said Max. "They might not be able to see you, but you can definitely see them. Come with me."

He began to run away from Megan. "Come on," he shouted over his shoulder, "I'll show you."

Megan looked at Jessie. "Is he telling me the truth?" said Megan. "Will I really be able to see my family?" she asked.

"Of course you will," said Jessie. "Now go and follow Max and he will show you what to do."

As Megan ran, she felt like a pup. She couldn't remember the last time she'd run anywhere. Now she felt like she had springs in her paws. She was like a springy, excitable puppy, bouncing through the grass, yapping and excited for the first time in so long. Max ran on ahead and Megan shouted, "Wait for me!" and she bounded off into the distance, excited to see what Max had to show her.

She caught him up at a huge lake filled with crystal blue water that glistened in the sunshine. It was so beautiful and as the birds flew about in the sky, she noticed that around the lake were other dogs, cats and rabbits, hamsters and guinea pigs and every other kind of animal she had ever seen before, and even some she'd never seen. All the animals were sat at the water's edge and were gently placing their paws in the water. "Come on," said Max, "let's find a spot," as he ran towards the water's edge.

Megan didn't much like water and was a bit concerned. "I'm not having a bath," she shouted after Max, "I don't like baths."

Max stopped and turned round. "Megan, it's not a bath, it's the Lake of Love. Now come on."

'The Lake of Love?' thought Megan, as she ran towards Max. She found him sat beside the water's edge. As she sat down she noticed that rather than grass, the entire area was covered in the most delicate, pure white feathers. She noticed the other animals were touching the water to make it ripple and were picking up feathers, kissing them and dropping them into the water.

"Why is everyone throwing feathers in the water, Max?"

Max looked at Megan and said, "Watch me." He leant over the water's edge and gently placed his paw in the water. A gentle ripple ran along the lake, and as the ripple cleared he turned to Megan and said, "Look." Hesitantly she peered into the water, and then she saw them: her Mummy and Daddy and Poppy and Louie, sitting together on the sofa, holding each other close and crying. It made her sad. Her leaving had done that.

"Choose a feather," said Max. "Choose a special feather, give it a gentle kiss and then throw it into the water. And then we wait."

Megan did as Max had said, and after gently kissing the feather and whispering, "I love you," she placed the feather on the water, but rather than floating away, it disappeared. "Where did it go?" said Megan. "Shouldn't feathers float?"

"These are special feathers," said Max. "They are feathers of love to let those we left behind know that we are always thinking of them."

"What do we do now?" asked Megan.

"Shh," said Max, "watch and listen." He leant towards the water and tapped it with his paw once more. "Watch this," he said to Megan, and as they leant over the water they saw Mummy and Daddy's house appear as though they were watching a film in the water. Mummy was standing looking out of the kitchen window and she looked so sad. Daddy was sat in the lounge on his chair reading the paper, still with tears on his cheeks. Poppy and Louie were sat on the sofa watching television looking very sad. And then it happened. The feather arrived. Max and Megan watched as it drifted into the kitchen and landed right beside Mummy. They watched her as she picked up the feather. She cried and shouted for everyone to come quick. And Megan and Max watched as they all hugged each other and cried, knowing that the feather was a message to say that Megan was safe, that she had travelled on her journey and she had arrived at Rainbow Bridge to be with Max.

It was then that Megan remembered all those years ago, when Mummy and Poppy and Louie used to place feathers beside Max's photograph on the fireplace. She realised that those feathers were Max letting them know he was okay and for them not to worry.

Suddenly, being away from her family didn't feel so bad for Megan. "How often can we come here?" she asked Max.

"Whenever you want," he said. "You can always come to the Lake of Love to see Mummy and Daddy and Poppy and Louie."

"And can we always send feathers?" she asked.

Max nodded. "Yes you can, but the best time to send down a feather is when you can see that they are sad, or having a bad day, because that feather will make them feel comforted to know we are thinking about them."

Megan was suddenly worried. "Do you think they will get another dog and forget about me?" Megan asked.

"They might get another dog," said Max, "and if they do, we will send down a feather to let them know that we are happy for them. But they will never forget us. I mean, did they forget me?"

Megan smiled and said, "No, they talked about you all the time."

Max cuddled into her and said, "And they will do the same for you."

Megan and Max sat beside one another, happy to be together again. It was getting dark, and Megan was still a little tired from her long journey to Rainbow Bridge. "Will I be able to sleep soon?" she asked Max. "Yes, later," he said, "but first we have to go and welcome Chip."

Megan looked confused again. "Who's Chip?"

"He's a dog," said Max, "and he's on his journey to Rainbow Bridge."

"But why do we have to go and meet him?" said Megan.

"Because he doesn't know anyone at Rainbow Bridge, so we need to make sure he doesn't feel alone."

Megan ran behind Max. "Are there lots of families like us at Rainbow Bridge, Max?" she asked as she caught up with him.

"We're all one big family, Megan," Max said, "and we all take care of each other."

And with that, they ran off towards the bridge, happy to be together, and happy to know that Mummy and Daddy and Poppy and Louie were never too far away.

CPSIA information can be obtained
at www.ICGtesting.com
Printed in the USA
BVHW021749200319
543218BV00008B/89/P

9 781911 113812